DRAGONFLY ON MY LINE

By: Gregory Guyton

To order additional copies of this book, contact:
Xlibris
844-714-8691
www.Xlibris.com
Orders@Xlibris.com

ISBN: Softcover   978-1-6698-0975-3
        Hardcover   978-1-6698-0974-6
        EBook   978-1-6698-0976-0

Print information available on the last page

Rev. date: 01/31/2022

DRAGONFLY ON MY LINE

IT'S SATURDAY MORNING
DADDY'S UP BEFORE DAY
I HEAR FOOTSTEPS WALKING
IN THE HALLWAY

I SMELL COFFEE BREWING
A LIGHT UNDER MY DOOR GLEEM
THIS COULD ONLY
MEAN ONE THING

DADDY OPEN'S MY DOOR
AND WITH A SMILE I HEAR HIM SAY
WAKE UP SON
WE'RE GOING FISHING TODAY

I JUMP FROM MY BED
MY FEET BARELY HITTING THE FLOOR
BEFORE I'M IN MY FISHING GEAR
AND HALFWAY OUT THE DOOR

MAMA KISSES MY CHEEK
OK BOYS, HAVE A GOOD DAY
DADDY GRABS OUR BAG LUNCH
AND WE'RE ON OUR WAY

WE DRIVE THROUGH TOWN
THE TRIFFIC LIGHTS ARE STILL BLINKING
DADDY DRINKS HIS COFFEE
AND I SIT BESIDE HIM THINKING

I WONDER IF
I'LL GET A BITE
EVEN IF I DON'T
IT'LL BE ALRIGHT

I WONDER IF DADDY WILL
LET ME STEER THE TRUCK
ONCE WE'RE FAR ENOUGH
OUT OF SIGHT

I WONDER IF
SOMEONE WILL BE
IN OUR FAVORITE SPOT
LIKE THEY WERE LAST TIME

I WONDER IF
A DRAGONFLY
WILL LAND
ON MY LINE

MY FAVORITE PART ABOUT FISHING
IS THE DRAGONFLIES I SEE
I TRIED TO CATCH ONE IN A JAR
BUT IT WAS MUCH TOO FAST FOR ME

DADDY SAYS THAT DRAGONFLIES
SOMETHIMES BRINGS US LUCK
AND IF ONE LANDS ON YOUR LINE
YOU'LL GET A BITE NO MATTER WHAT

I OFTEN WONDER HOW THEY FLY
SO SWIFTLY THROUGH THE AIR
THEY MOVE SO FAST THAT IF YOU BLINK
THEY MAY NOT BE THERE

I LOVE TO SEE THEM IN A GROUP
OF THREE, SIX OR NINE
OH BOY I HOPE A DRAGONFLY
LANDS ON MY LINE

WE PULL UP TO OUR FAVORITE SPOT
NOT ANOTHER PERSON IN SIGHT
THE WATER IS CALM ON THE LITTLE POND
AND EVERYTHING SEEMS ALRIGHT

BY NOW THE SUN'S JUST SHOWING HIS FACE
FROM BEHIND SOME TALL PINE TREES
I JUMP FROM THE TRUCK GRAB MY POLE AND HAT
THE GRASS IS UP TO MY KNEES

WE WALK TOWARD THE POND
NO DRAGONFLIES YET
BUT THEY'LL BE AROUND
PRETTY SOON I BET

WE FISH FOR A WHILE
DADDY PULLS IN A BASS
I HOOK A SMALL GUPPY
THAT GETS STUCK IN THE GRASS

I TRY ONCE AGAIN
I LET DADDY BAIT MY HOOK
THOSE LITTLE WORMS ARE TRICKY
AND I DON'T CARE FOR HOW THEY LOOK

STILL NO SIGN OF A DRAGONFLY
I THINK I NEED A LITTLE LUCK
DADDY CATCHES TWO MORE
BEFORE I REALIZE MY HOOK IS STUCK

BUT DO I MIND
NO WAY NOT ME
BECAUSE THEIR'S ONLY ONE THING
I'M HERE TO SEE

IT STARTS WITH A "D"
AND ENDS WITH A "Y"
CAN YOU GUESS WHAT IT IS
YEP, A DRAGONFLY

DADDY LOOKS AT ME
AS I STARE IN THE SKY
WISHING AND PRAYING
TO SEE A DRAGONFLY

YOU MUST BE PATIENT SON
GOOD THINGS COME TO THOES WHO WAIT
IF YOU WANT TO CATCH A FISH
YOU MUST FIRST CONCENTRATE

BUT LITTLE DOES HE KNOW
A FISH IS THE LAST THING ON MY MIND
I'D RATHER SEE A DRAGONFLY
LAND ON MY LINE

BY NOW THE SUN IS HIGH IN THE SKY
AND WE BREAK TO HAVE A SNACK
DADDY PULLS BOLOGNA SANDWICHES
FROM OUR LUNCH SACK

WE LAY BACK ON THE GRASS
AND LOOK UP AT THE CLOUDS
I THINK THAT IF I CAUGHT A FISH
MY DADDY WOULD BE PROUD

I CAN SEE ALL TYPES OF ANIMALS
FLOATING ACROSS THE SKY
I BET IF I TRIED REALLY HARD
I COULD MAKE OUT A DRAGONFLY

WE DRINK GRAPE SODA
AND EAT POTATO CHIPS TOO
BEFORE LONG AN HOUR PASSED
PRETTY SOON ANOTHER DOES TOO

WE ALWAYS HAVE FUN
MY DADDY AND ME
WHEATHER FISHING, HUNTING, BOWLING
OR JUST WATCHING TV

I HEAR DADDY'S FISH SPLASHING
IN A PAIL NEAR MY FEET
WE MOVE TO A DIFFERENT SPOT
TO AVOID THE SUMMER HEAT

JUST AS I THOW IN MY HOOK
I FEEL A TUG ON MY LINE
I YELL OUT **DADDY LOOK**
I THINK I GOT ONE THIS TIME

I REELLED IT IN SLOW
TRYING NOT TO GO TOO FAST
I GOT IT TO THE EDGE
AND STAYED AWAY FROM THE GRASS

I DID JUST AS DADDY SAID
AND I TRIED TO CONCENTRATE
I GET IT ALL THE WAY TO THE EDGE
AND THE FEELING IS **GREAT!**

I PULL MY LINE UP OVER THE GRASS
BUT I TRIP OVER DADDY'S PAIL
MY POLE WENT UP AND I WENT DOWN
AND UP POPS A TURTLE SHELL

WITH FOUR LITTLE LEGS
WAVING AND FLAPPING
KICKING FOR DEAR LIFE
TWISTING AND SNAPPING

DADDY LETS OUT A LAUGH
AND I START TO LAUGH TOO
DADDY SAYS WE CAN THROW HIM BACK
OR WOULD YOU LIKE SOME TURTLE STEW

I PUT MY POLE ON THE GROUND
AND TOOK THE HOOK OUT HIS SHELL
AFTER THAT I SET HIM FREE
AND HE WAS HAPPY, I COULD TELL

HE CRAWLED BACK INTO THE LITTLE POND
JUST AS FAST AS HE COULD
AS DADDY PULLS IN ANOTHER FISH
AND ANOTHER, AND ANOTHER HE WOULD

I THROW IN MY LINE
ONCE AGAIN
IN HOPES OF SOME LUCK
FROM A LITTLE FRIEND

AS I WATCH MY CORK SIT
STILL ON THE WATER
I SEE THE REFLECTION OF THE SKY
AND I CONCENTRATE HARDER

I WAS JUST ABOUT TO GIVE UP
WHEN I HEARD MY DADDY SAY
LOOK SON IS THAT A DRAGONFLY
COMING THIS WAY

I STARTED NOT TO
LIFT MY HEAD
CAUSE I THOUGHT DADDY
WAS JUST PULLING MY LEG

I THOUGHT THAT HE
WOULD MAKE ME LOOK
ONLY TO SAY
JUST KIDDING INSTEAD

BUT GUESS WHAT
IT WAS TRUE
AND NOT ONLY ONE
THEIR WERE TWO

OH ME, OH MY
OH MY, OH ME
THEIR HEADED STRIGHT
TOWARD ME

NOT ONE BUT TWO
TO BRING ME LUCK
NO MORE TURTLES AND
GUPPIES TO MESS THINGS UP

I'M GOING TO CATCH A GIANT
OF A FISH THIS TIME
JUST AS SOON AS A DRAGONFLY
LANDS ON MY LINE

SO I HAVE TO BE CARFUL
NOT TO SCARE THEM AWAY
I STAND VERY STILL
AND NOT A WORD DO I SAY

IT FLIES OVER MY HEAD
JUST AS FAST AS THE WIND
THEN CIRCLES AROUND
AND COMES BACK AGAIN

IT LANDS ON A ROCK
IT LANDS ON A LILLYPAD
IT LANDS ON DADDY'S LINE
THAT SORTA MADE ME MAD

BUT WHEN I TURNED AGAIN
AND LOOKED AT MY LINE
CAN YOU GUESS WHAT WAS THERE
SITTING ON MINE

A DRAGONFLY, A DRAGONFLY
MY WISH CAME TRUE
OH DRAGONFLY, DRAGONFLY
HOW I LOVE YOU

I WANTED TO CATCH IT
AND TAKE IT HOME
TO KEEP IN
MY ROOM

THEN I RMEMBERED
WITH HIM ON MY LINE
I'D CATCH A FISH
PRETTY SOON

DADDY LOOKED AT THE DRAGONFLY
THEN LOOKED AT ME
AND GAVE A SMILE AS TO SAY
NOW LET'S SEE

AND THEN IN A SECOND
I DECLARE IT COULDN'T
HAVE BEEN
MUCH MORE

SOMETHING HAPPENED
TO MY POLE
THAT HADN'T
HAPPENED BEFORE

IT STARTED TO BEND
IT STARTED TO SHAKE
I EVEN THOUGHT
THAT IT WOULD BREAK

DADDY'S EYES GOT WIDE
MY HEART STARTED TO RACE
THIS WAS SOMETHING BIG
I COULD TELL BY HIS FACE

HE DROPPED HIS POLE
TO HELP ME BRING IT IN
THE DRAGONFLY FLEW AWAY
AND THE STRUGGLE BEGAN

BUT WITH DADDY'S HELP
A LITTLE LUCK
AND
A WISH

I MANAGED
TO CATCH
A MEGA
CATFISH

IT WAS A WOPPER
THE BIGGEST FISH
MY EYES
HAD EVER SEEN

IT COULD BARELY
FIT IN THE BUCKET
WITH DADDY'S FISH
I MEAN THE THING

WAS AS LONG AS I WAS
WITH SHARP TINY TEETH
IT WEIGHED 100 POUNDS
IT WAS BEYOND BELIEF

MY DADDY WAS HAPPY
HE CHEERED OUT LOUD
HE COULDN'T BELIEVE IT EITHER
I COULD TELL HE WAS PROUD

I CAUGHT FOUR MORE FISH
THAT VERY SAME DAY
AND I BAITED MY OWN HOOK TOO
BY THE WAY

IT WAS GETTING LATE
SO WE HEADED HOME
THE SKY LOOKED LIKE
IT WOULD RAIN

THE SUN WAS SLEEPY
AND STARTED TO FALL
AND CRICKETS BEGAN
TO SANG

AND THE SAME DRAGONFLIES
THAT BROUGHT US LUCK
FOLLOWED DADDY AND I
ALL THE WAY TO THE TRUCK

NOW I HAVE ANOTHER REASON
FOR LOVING THEM SO
DRAGONFLIES ARE LUCKY
NOW I KNOW

WHEN WE GOT HOME
MAMA GREETED US AT THE DOOR
DID YOU CATCH ANYTHING
OR WAS THE DAY ONE BIG BORE

DADDY AND I
DIDN'T SAY A THING
WE JUST SHOWED HER
A BIG BUCKET OF FISH TO CLEAN

WHEN SHE ASKED
WHO CAUGHT THIS GAINT CATFISH
I SIMPLY SMILED AND SAID
I GOT MY WISH

WE TOLD HER ALL ABOUT
THE WONDER DAY WE HAD
AND I CAN'T WAIT TO GO FISHING AGAIN
JUST ME AND MY DAD

Printed in the United States
by Baker & Taylor Publisher Services